AND THE
SECRET DOOR

The Junior Novelization

Special thanks to Diane Reichenberger, Cindy Ledermann, Sarah Lazar, Charnita Belcher, Tanya Mann, Julia Phelps, Nicole Corse, Sharon Woloszyk, Rita Lichtwardt, Carla Alford, Renee Reeser Zelnick, Rob Hudnut, David Wiebe, Shelley Dvi-Vardhana, Gabrielle Miles, Rainmaker Entertainment, and Walter P. Martishius

Published in the United States by Random House Children's Books, a division of Random House LLC, 1745 Broadway, New York, NY 10019, and in Canada by Random House of Canada Limited, Toronto, Penguin Random House Companies. Random House and the colophon are registered trademarks of Random House LLC.
ISBN 978-0-385-38627-2 (pbk) — ISBN 978-0-385-38628-9 (ebook)
randomhouse.com/kids
Printed in the United States of America
10 9 8 7 6 5 4 3 2 1
First Edition

The Junior Novelization

Adapted by Molly McGuire Woods

Based on the original screenplay by
Brian Hohlfeld

Illustrated by Ulkutay Design Group

Random House 🏠 New York

Who's Who and What's What

Alexa: the princess of a large kingdom. She is intimidated by the duties of a princess and would much rather read than dance at a ball or give a royal speech. But when she discovers magical powers in the kingdom of Zinnia, she learns that she's capable of much more than she thought.

Brookhurst: Princess Alexa's butler. He makes sure Alexa follows her royal schedule— or at least, he tries to.

Grandmother: Alexa's grandmother. She passed her love of reading on to Alexa.

Grodlin: Princess Malucia's trog attendant. He is put in charge of Malucia while her parents are away, but he is unable to keep her out of trouble.

The Grove: a floating island in the trees of Zinnia where Romy, Nori, and other magical creatures hide from Princess Malucia.

Hilgovia: a neighboring kingdom that is invited to the royal ball.

Jenna: one of Alexa's best friends. A great dancer, Jenna is always ready to help Alexa with her dance moves.

King Terrance: Alexa's father.

King and Queen of Zinnia: Malucia's parents. They spoil their daughter and let her do whatever she wants.

Malucia: the spoiled princess of Zinnia. She has no magical powers of her own, so she steals magic from the rest of the kingdom and tries to rule it while her parents are away.

Mr. Primrose: the royal dance instructor. He tries his best to teach Alexa but ends up getting hurt in the process.

Nola: a tiny fairy who lives in Zinnia. Malucia steals her magic.

Nori: a fairy who lives in Zinnia and becomes a loyal friend to Alexa.

Prince Kieran: the Prince of Hilgovia.

Queen Adrienne: Alexa's mother. She loves tradition and encourages Alexa to embrace her role as princess.

The Queen Unicorn: the most magical unicorn in Zinnia. She must be protected from Princess Malucia.

Romy: a mermaid who lives in Zinnia and becomes a loyal friend to Alexa.

Royal Ball: a palace tradition for the past 160 years. It always begins with the princess dancing a waltz.

Samantha: one of Alexa's best friends and a great dancer. She loves hip-hop music but is amazing at dancing the waltz, too.

Scepter: a long rod carried by royalty. Malucia uses hers to steal and store magic from other creatures in Zinnia.

Sniff & Whiff: sniffers who work for Princess Malucia.

Sniffers: creatures that can detect magic by smell.

Stenchweed: an herb that hides the scent of magic.

Trogs: Princess Malucia's guards.

Waltz: a ballroom dance performed by a couple who turn as a pair around the dance floor.

Zinnia: a magical kingdom accessed through a secret door in Alexa's garden.

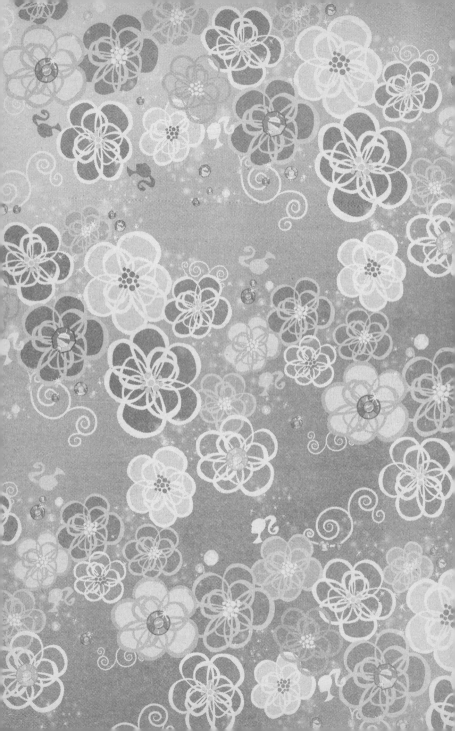

Chapter 1

Princess Alexa moved a stack of books and plopped into the armchair in her room. She swung her legs over the side and twisted her blond hair back with a long hair stick. Then she opened her newest book and sighed happily.

There was nothing she loved more than escaping from her royal duties with a good story. Being a princess was hard work—there were so many expectations. In a book, you could be anything you wanted to be. Some days, Alexa wished she were anything but a princess.

Just as she began to read, there was a knock on her bedroom door.

"Princess Alexa? Are you in there?" a man asked from the other side.

Alexa recognized her butler's voice. "In here, Brookhurst!" she called. She made her way to the door.

"Sorry to interrupt, Your Highness," said Brookhurst.

"No problem," Alexa replied, closing her book. "How can I help you?"

"The Equestrian Club has asked if you might say a few words before their exhibition this afternoon," he said.

Alexa bit her lip. "You mean . . . a speech?" Speaking in front of people made her nervous. As a princess, she was asked to make a lot of speeches. That was part of the reason she sometimes wished she weren't a princess. "Not just for the horses, I'm guessing?" she joked.

Brookhurst gave her a kind smile. "I believe the two-legged members of the club will be there as well, Your Highness."

"Of course," Alexa said, wringing her hands. "Please thank them for the invitation, but . . ."

"But you send your regrets," the butler said, finishing her sentence. It wasn't the first time Alexa had declined an invitation to make a public appearance. It just made her so anxious to think of all those people staring at her.

What if she didn't say the right thing or act the right way? A princess was supposed to be perfect—and Alexa felt anything but.

Brookhurst bowed as he exited, leaving Alexa alone with her thoughts.

"A speech?" she muttered under her breath. "I can't do that." She twirled around the room, hugging her book to her chest. Books never made her feel uncomfortable or asked her to give speeches. In books, Alexa could be whoever she wanted.

There was another knock.

Brookhurst stood in the open doorway. "Princess Alexa, the Prince of Hilgovia has arrived for tea. Your grandmother says she would be very pleased if you would join them."

"Um . . ." Alexa hesitated, trying to think of an excuse. "Maybe it would be better if you—"

"—just say hello for you," Brookhurst concluded. "Of course, Your Highness."

As he closed the door, Alexa flopped onto her bed. If only she had a whole day to hide in her room and read! Better yet, she wished she could *be* a character in one of her books. They always seemed to have all the answers.

The sound of her mother's approaching footsteps snapped Alexa out of her daydream.

"The dance instructor is waiting," the queen said sternly when she reached her daughter's room. "And so are your friends."

Alexa glanced at the clock. She had almost forgotten about her dance lesson—or rather, she wished she could forget about it. There was a royal ball tonight! Everyone expected her to waltz in front of a huge audience. It was tradition. But so far, Alexa had been too nervous about it to get any of the steps right in rehearsals. She felt like she was going to make a fool of herself in front of the whole kingdom.

"Oh . . . well . . . ," she said, stalling.

"No more excuses," her mother declared. "The ball is tonight. You must finally learn to dance like a princess. Come now."

Alexa heaved a sigh and followed her mother down the hall.

Chapter 2

Alexa peeked into the palace ballroom. She spotted her friends Jenna and Samantha. They were practicing a modern dance routine they had made up themselves.

"Five, six, seven, eight," Jenna counted.

Their instructor, Mr. Primrose tapped his watch. "Girls, girls," he scolded. "We are here to practice the art of the dance, not that hippity-hop!"

Jenna and Samantha dissolved in giggles.

Alexa entered the room. "Sorry I'm late, Mr. Primrose," she said, waving hello to the girls.

"Princess Alexa, how delightful of you to join

us," Mr. Primrose said sarcastically. "Let's pick up where we left off last session, shall we?" He positioned Jenna and Samantha on either side of Alexa. "The ladies-in-waiting stand here, um, waiting. Then your father, the king, bows to you, the princess." Mr. Primrose bowed to Alexa, showing her how it would look. Then he took her hand. "The orchestra begins." He closed his eyes as he pictured the spectacle of it all.

The queen started the music. Alexa took a deep breath, getting ready to practice. But instead of the sweeping classical waltz they all expected, the thumping base of a hip-hop song blasted through the speakers. *Thump-thumpity-bump!*

Samantha burst into giggles, and Jenna shook her head in embarrassment. Alexa couldn't help but laugh. Samantha was always up to something silly—and it sure did help break the tension!

The queen frowned and found the correct track to play. As the waltz music filled the air, Alexa's nerves returned.

Mr. Primrose led her around the floor. "And

one-two-three, one-two-three. Eyes up, Your Highness," he instructed her.

Alexa tried to stop watching her feet, but that made her dizzy!

"Mr. Primrose," she protested, "this really isn't my thing."

"Nonsense, Your Highness," Mr. Primrose replied, twirling her faster. "Just glide-two-three, glide-two-three."

Alexa sighed. It seemed no matter how many times she tried to explain herself, no one ever really listened. "You're very patient," she continued. "But I'm afraid I'm not—"

"No, no, you're doing *exceedingly* well, Your Highness. One-two-WHOA!"

Alexa had stepped on Mr. Primrose's foot. *Crash!* He fell to the floor.

"Oh!" Alexa cried, dropping to his side. "I'm so sorry. Oh, dear, Mr. Primrose." She helped him hobble to a nearby chair.

"Ah, yes," the dance instructor winced, rubbing his ankle. "Well, that's a bit tender."

Alexa felt terrible. Not only was she a poor

dancer, but she'd really hurt someone!

"Mother, " she said, turning to face the queen. "I've tried to learn the dance, but—I just can't. I better sit this one out."

The queen shook her head. "Nonsense," she said with a wave of her hand. "It's tradition! Every royal ball for the last one hundred fifty—"

"One hundred *sixty*," Mr. Primrose corrected her.

"—*sixty* years—has begun with this waltz. And now that you're seventeen, it's your turn to carry on the tradition."

Alexa hung her head. Everyone was so concerned with tradition. But what if she just didn't fit the part? "Everybody will be *watching* me," she said miserably.

The queen heaved a sigh. "That is the general idea, Alexa," she explained. "After all, you *are* the princess."

"Um, Your Majesty?" Jenna asked, waving her arm to get the queen's attention. "I could do the waltz at the ball instead of Alexa!"

Alexa clapped her hands together. "That's a

great idea!" She knew that Jenna loved to be center stage. This way they would both win!

The queen crossed her arms. "Thank you, Jenna," she said sternly. "But Princess Alexa must be the one to dance."

Jenna shrugged. "Worth a try," she whispered to Alexa under her breath.

"If you don't mind, Your Highness," Mr. Primrose said from his chair, "I think I'd better see to my ankle."

The queen nodded. "Brookhurst," she called. "Help me with Mr. Primrose, please?" The butler and the queen offered Mr. Primrose their arms and assisted him from the room.

"Jenna, Samantha," the queen called over her shoulder. "*Please* show Alexa how to do the dance, would you?"

Chapter 3

Alexa rolled her eyes when her mother had left the room. "Sorry you guys have to do this," she said to her friends.

"Are you kidding?" Jenna said, doing a little dance. "It means getting to wear an amazing dress tonight."

"Wait a sec—" Samantha began, a twinkle in her eye. "The queen didn't say *which* dance, did she?" She pulled another music track from her bag and popped it in. "Remember this?" she asked as a dance beat thumped through the air. She started to move, and Jenna joined in. It was obvious they knew this routine well.

"Come on, Alexa!" Jenna urged.

Alexa shuffled her foot nervously. "Uhh, I don't know. I can't dance like you guys."

"Try it!" Jenna said. "Like we showed you last time! Five, six, seven, eight."

Alexa hesitated, but then she copied Jenna's steps. She realized she could keep time to the music and follow her friends' steps. She was *dancing*—and it felt pretty good! But then she lost her concentration and tripped. "Sorry—I can't keep up with you!" she cried, feeling defeated.

"You were doing great," Samantha told her.

Alexa shook her head. "I'm having enough trouble learning the waltz."

Samantha put a hand on her hip. "Alexa, you're a princess. Which means you're good at *everything*!" she teased.

Alexa gave an uncomfortable laugh. "So everyone keeps telling me."

"Don't worry. You'll do great," Jenna said, putting an arm around her shoulder.

"Thanks, guys," Alexa replied. She gathered

her things and waved to her friends. "I'll see you tonight."

Lost in thought, the princess practically bumped into her grandmother on the way out of the ballroom.

"*I* thought you danced beautifully," her grandmother said, cupping Alexa's chin in her palm.

Alexa hugged her grandmother. "You *have* to say that," she joked. "You're my grandmother."

Alexa followed her grandmother down the hall to a sitting room.

"You shouldn't hide your talents, dear. What are you afraid of?" her grandmother asked gently.

Alexa blew out a frustrated breath. "Other than an epic fail in front of everyone?" she asked.

Her grandmother chuckled and took her hand. "I do wish you had come to tea. The Prince of Hilgovia is very nice. And he's your age."

Alexa rolled her eyes. "Grandma, you know I don't like that stuff. Meeting people, giving speeches, going to balls ... ."

"All those horrible things princesses are

forced to do," her grandmother kidded.

"Grandma!" Alexa cried, trying hard not to smile.

"Princess or not," her grandmother continued. "You can't hide from life forever, dear. You'll never know what you're good at unless you try. Here." She pushed a book across the table. "I brought this for you."

"But I've read all your books, Grandma."

"Not this one," her grandmother replied. "I've been saving it for the right time." She opened the book and read the first line. "'In a kingdom by the sea lived a princess who had magical powers.'" She paused and looked at Alexa, her eyes shining with mischief. "Ah, but you probably wouldn't like it."

"Grandma!" Alexa cried, reaching eagerly for the book. "Thanks. You know exactly what I like." She headed back down the hall, opening the book along the way.

 # Chapter 4

Alexa wandered down a garden path, reading out loud as she went.

"'The princess could have made flowers bloom or changed the color of her dress. But you can't use magic if you don't know you have it.'"

Alexa eyed her own dress curiously. She held up her pointer finger like it was a magic wand and shook it.

"Pink!" she exclaimed. But of course, her dress didn't change a bit. Alexa giggled at her own silliness and continued reading.

"'In the wall of her garden was a door she

had never noticed before, a door that led to a fantastic world that she would never forget.' "

Alexa sat on a low-hanging tree branch. She continued reading. " 'With a flick of a wand, she discovered—she had magic!' "

Alexa closed the book and hugged it to her chest. She thought about how amazing it would be to really, truly possess magic. She imagined all of the things she could do with it—not just changing the color of her dress. She could help people—maybe she could even help herself be less nervous.

She moved through the garden, daydreaming about a life full of magic.

She reached a high, ivy-covered wall at the edge of the garden. Through the ivy she noticed a sparkling arched door. Alexa didn't remember ever seeing this door before, yet it somehow looked familiar.

Quickly, she fumbled to a page in her book with a drawing of a doorway on it. She held it up to the wall and compared the two. They looked the same!

"Huh," Alexa said curiously.

She placed the book on the grass nearby and touched the door's handle. Then she hesitated. What could be on the other side? She thought of her grandmother's words: She would never know unless she tried.

Here goes nothing, Alexa thought. She pushed gently on the handle, and the door opened. A glittering glow of sparkles surprised her.

"Whoa!" she yelped, peering through the doorway. A colorful tunnel stretched out before her. She took a tentative step inside. There was no telling what lay ahead.

Suddenly worried, Alexa stepped back into the garden and closed the door. Then she heard Brookhurst's voice.

"Your Highness! Good news! Mr. Primrose is recovering. You may continue the dance lesson."

Alexa held her breath. She didn't want to go back to practicing. Before she could talk herself out of it, Alexa threw open the hidden door and stepped inside.

Chapter 5

A tunnel stretched out in front of Alexa. Its walls shimmered and sparkled with vibrant colors. They seemed to be beckoning Alexa forward. Overhead she spied a trellis, thick with lush, exotic plants. Alexa took one step forward and then another. As she walked, the tunnel curved and the colors glowed brighter and brighter with each step.

Alexa wasn't sure where this passageway led, but she felt certain that something special lay at the other end.

Finally, Alexa reached the archway at the end of the tunnel. Shielding her eyes, she stepped into the bright sunlight and gasped. A flourishing, brilliant landscape stretched out before her in every direction. What a remarkable place!

Plants of dazzling colors wound their way over rocks and through trees, reaching high into the sky. Neon-colored vines swirled around tree trunks and climbed upward.

Even the grass was somehow lit from within, glowing a beautiful aquamarine. Flowers and bushes—some larger than Alexa's head—seemed suspended in midair!

It was as if someone had planted a group of gardens and set them drifting through the air like a bunch of rainbow-hued balloons! Alexa couldn't explain it—the whole effect was magical!

A stream wound its way through the foliage, pleasantly babbling as it went. A small, fantastical purple creature bounced on its curly tail past Alexa's feet. It hopped onto a floating garden, two similar creatures following behind it.

Alexa chuckled. Everything felt so new and wonderfully exciting!

Just then she heard a sound. *Whirr-thunk!*

An arrow landed in a tree trunk next to her.

"Ahh!" she cried, glancing around to see who could have shot it her way.

"Intruder!" a voice called from over the hill.

Alexa looked for a place to hide.

"We know you're there!" came another voice, this one closer.

Alexa ducked behind a bush as two figures came over the hill. They looked like girls about her age—only something was different. Their clothes, decorated with shells and butterflies, seemed more suited for a fairy tale—as if they were magical creatures.

Oddly, it also seemed to Alexa that they weren't quite sure how to walk on the ground. *Strange,* she thought.

Then one of the girls strung another arrow into a slender bow. Alexa hid.

"You might as well swim out," said the strawberry-blond archer. She and her brunette friend inched their way toward Alexa's hiding spot.

Alexa ventured another peek through the branches. "Swim?" she asked.

"Show yourself," commanded the brunette. She sounded stern.

The archer tripped clumsily. "Whoa! Ahhh, legs!" she cried, righting herself.

"Just come out!" huffed the brunette.

Alexa bit her lip. She didn't have much choice. After all, she was a stranger here—not to mention the fact that she didn't have a bow and arrow. Alexa crept out from under the bush. She nervously brushed leaves from her dress.

The two girls looked her up and down, examining her.

"Who are you and— Wait. A tiara? Are you a princess?" asked the brunette.

"I'm Princess Alexa," she said, bending to curtsey.

As she did, she noticed that her clothes had changed completely! Her everyday dress was gone, and in its place she wore a glittering gown of neon pink.

How had this happened?

Chapter 6

Alexa glanced in the direction of the tunnel and scratched her head.

In front of her, the two girls dropped to their knees, in the clumsiest curtsies Alexa had ever seen. They tried to address her properly.

"Your Highness, my name is Nori," said the brunette seriously.

"And my name is Romy, Your Princessness," the archer said, flopping to the ground in a dramatic curtsey.

Princess Alexa stifled a laugh. "I'm sorry," she said shyly. "Maybe I should just go back the way I came and—"

"No! Stay!" Nori said.

Romy jumped up from the ground. "You can help us!" she cried eagerly. Then she turned to Nori. "She can help us!"

Alexa looked from one girl to the other, confused. "Wh-what are you talking about? Help with what?"

"Well." Nori sighed, unsure how to begin. Then she told Alexa about a princess named Malucia.

Malucia's parents ruled the kingdom of Zinnia with magic and love. But Malucia had been born without magic—in a kingdom where everyone else had it. The princess decided that if she couldn't make magic of her own, she would take it from others.

So she waited for her parents to go on a trip. Then she began terrorizing the land with her army, stealing the magical powers of all the creatures she could get her hands on.

"She took my wings away," Nori continued, explaining that she used to be a fairy, free to flutter wherever she pleased. "But now our luck will change because you're here."

Alexa shook her head. "I'm still not sure what you think I can do," she said.

"Malucia came and took my tail away," Romy said, hanging her head sadly. "No more swimming for me."

"I'm so sorry. That's horrible!" Alexa exclaimed. "Are you a fish?"

Romy laughed. "No, a mermaid!" she declared.

Everything was starting to make sense to Alexa. No wonder Nori and Romy seemed so unsure on their feet—they were used to flying and swimming instead. And in their world, princesses had magic, which was why they thought she could help.

There was just one problem: Alexa wasn't from their world, so she didn't have magic.

"Now that you're here, all our problems will disappear," Romy continued.

Nori signaled to the bushes nearby.

Before Alexa knew it, she was surrounded by fairies of all different sizes. Even some mermaids swam to the side of the river. They all wanted to see the princess who had come to save the day.

"Your Highness, you're the only one who can rescue us," Nori declared.

Alexa was sure Nori and Romy were joking. But as they stared at her expectantly, Alexa began to realize they were serious.

She had no idea what to do.

Chapter 7

Alexa took a step back. "Look," she said, as firmly as she could. "I'm very sorry to hear about this Malucia and what she did to you. But I can't help anyone."

Romy waved her hand through the air. "Well, sure you can!"

"With your magic!" cried Nori.

The fairies all around them nodded.

"I hate to disappoint you," Alexa continued. "But I don't have any magic."

Nori and Romy looked confused.

"So you don't know about that *wand* in your hair?" Romy asked, chuckling.

Now it was Alexa's turn to look confused. "Wand?" She reached up and pulled out her hair stick. Sure enough, just like her dress had transformed, her hair stick was now a golden wand with a sparkling gem on top! She shook her head in disbelief. "I have no idea where this came from. Or the gown," she said.

"How else does a princess dress?" Nori asked, unconvinced.

Alexa thought for a minute. "Well, for hanging out around the castle, I usually wear something like . . . how can I describe it? It's sort of like . . ." She waved her wand absentmindedly.

Zing!

A beam of magic shot from her wand toward Nori. It knocked the wingless fairy to the ground.

"Oof!" Nori gasped.

Alexa rushed to her side. "Are you okay?"

Nori nodded. Then both girls looked at Nori's outfit. She wore the very same dress that Alexa had been wearing when she'd left the royal garden only moments earlier!

"Whoa-ho-ho!" Romy shouted.

"Ugh, yellow!" Nori exclaimed, eyeing the dress suspiciously.

"Wow," Alexa said. "Did I just do that?" She looked at her wand and wondered—was it really magic? There was only one way to find out.

"Let's see if I can change it back!" she suggested. She waved her wand through the air a few times. Nothing happened. "Hang on, I'll get it." She flicked her wand again and waited. Still nothing.

"If I hold it like this or . . . ?" But nothing seemed to work. Just as quickly as Alexa's magic had appeared, it seemed to have vanished.

One of the furry creatures Alexa had seen earlier bounced over to Nori. It gestured nervously. Nori held a hand to her ear. "Listen."

Alexa heard a *click-click*ing noise nearby.

"Oh no!" Romy cried.

"Sniffers!" Nori whispered. "Malucia's minions! They'll smell your magic!"

Romy grabbed Alexa's wand and lowered it. "Dive!" she called.

All of the mermaids, fairies, and creatures

scattered away, frightened and panicked.

"Romy! You get the princess to the grove, and I'll throw Sniff and Whiff off the scent," Nori commanded.

"Come on, Alexa!" Romy grabbed Alexa by the arm and pulled her through the brush, tripping as she went. "Ugh! Legs!" she cried.

Chapter 8

Alexa followed Romy as best she could, struggling to understand what was happening. Minions? Sniffers? Smelling magic?

She glanced over her shoulder and watched as Nori grabbed handfuls of leaves and herbs and scattered them on the ground.

"All right, sniffers, sniff *this*!" Nori called.

Romy and Alexa arrived at a large grove of thick trees. Nori joined them. They hid as two armadillo-like creatures rolled over the hill. They made a *click-click-click* sound as they moved about, sniffing Nori's herbs.

Romy tugged on a nearby vine and three long

silk ropes tumbled from the floating tree above.

"Here you go!" Romy said, swinging one of the ropes toward Alexa, who caught it in both hands.

"What's this?" Alexa asked, putting her foot in a loop at the bottom of the rope, like Romy. Then she grasped it with both hands and waited. Suddenly, the rope shot upward into the tree.

"Hold tight!" Nori said, grabbing hold of her own rope.

Alexa clung to the rope with all her might as it zoomed through branches and leaves, rising higher and higher. She had never been so far off the ground before.

This must be how it feels to fly like a fairy! Alexa thought.

The rope stopped by a wooden platform built into the tree branches like a tree house. Following Nori and Romy's lead, Alexa jumped onto the platform. The girls peered carefully over the edge.

Down below, the sniffers unrolled themselves to get a better scent around the base of the tree.

"Ugh! Stenchweed!" cried the sniffer with the purple face.

The green-faced sniffer rolled his eyes. "Well, yeah, Sniff! A one-nostriled dipthorn with a *cold* could have picked that up!"

"But wait, wait, wait, Whiff. On the end I'm getting a hint of berry." Sniff inhaled deeply. "And chocolate, leather undertones."

Whiff threw up his paws. "What? Now you're just making stuff up." He sniffed the ground. "I'm not getting any of that!"

"That's because your nose is shorter. Which is why Mom always liked me better," Sniff teased.

"You're just messing with me again," Whiff said, frowning. "She never said that. Did she?"

Sniff put his nose to the ground once more and concentrated on picking up a scent.

"You better find the unicorns or Malucia is going to turn you into a clodwinkle," Whiff warned.

"I better find them?" said Sniff. "Oh no, no,

no, *you* better find them, you clodwinkle."

"You're a clodwinkle!"

The sniffers continued arguing with one another as they rolled out of sight.

One thing was certain: they'd both be in trouble if they didn't find those unicorns for Malucia.

Chapter 9

Up in the treetop, Nori and Romy sighed with relief.

Alexa struggled to put it all together. "What were those?" she stammered.

"Sniffers," Nori replied. "They work for Princess Malucia. Let's go. We're almost home."

The three climbed farther up the tree and ventured onto a floating piece of land. It rested in the air above the canopy of trees—impossible to see from the ground.

"Home!" Romy exclaimed.

"A strategically camouflaged hideout," Nori said. "But, yeah, home."

Alexa took in her surroundings. The island was bustling with life and beautiful beyond words. Fairies, both big and small, buzzed about. They weaved in and out of branches and vines, gathering fruit or playing games.

"This is— I can't even— I love it!" Alexa cried, clasping her hands with delight.

Next, they walked through a canopy of branches to a clear, cool lagoon. It didn't make sense that a lagoon could simply be hanging between the trees—yet here it was, mermaids splashing around lily pads and resting on shore. Alexa was speechless—she had read about fairylands and magical kingdoms in her books. But seeing one firsthand was beyond her wildest dreams.

Nori motioned for the fairies, mermaids, and other woodland creatures to gather around. "Attention!" she began. "This is Princess Alexa."

"She's come to save us," Romy added.

The fairies and mermaids bowed to Alexa and chattered excitedly.

"We're saved!"

"Welcome, Your Highness!"

Alexa shuffled her foot nervously. How was she going to tell them that she didn't have the powers they thought she did?

Then some of the fairies noticed Nori's princess clothes and began to giggle.

Nori's face reddened. "Um, Princess Alexa, no one can take me seriously looking like this," she complained.

In all the excitement, Alexa had forgotten that Nori was still dressed in princess gear.

"Your clothes! Hmm. Let's see," she said, placing her finger on her chin. "When the magic worked before, I was thinking about what I usually wear. So maybe—if I think—and point—" She closed her eyes and waved her wand, all the while thinking about Nori's original clothes.

Zing!

A flash of pink magic zipped toward Nori. And her old clothes reappeared! The crowd gasped.

"Ah!" Nori exclaimed, relieved. "Thank you!"

"It worked!" Alexa cried.

Romy looked closely at Nori's shirt. "You even got rid of the embarrassing berry stain!" she joked.

"That *was* embarrassing," echoed a mermaid, chuckling.

Nori crossed her arms. "Hmph," she said, pouting. But Alexa could tell she was trying not to laugh along with her friends.

Just then, Alexa felt someone—or something—nudge her from behind. She turned to see a small purple unicorn nuzzling her shoulder.

"Wow. Hello there," Alexa said softly, patting the unicorn's nose. She had never seen a real live unicorn before. Talk about magic!

Two more unicorns stepped forward—a rose-colored one and another sky blue. "Unbelievable."

"Watch out, their horns are kind of sharp," Romy warned.

The purple unicorn brayed at Romy, offended.

"I'm sorry," Romy replied, holding up her hands in protest. "They are!"

"The fairies and mermaids have come together to protect the unicorns from Malucia," Nori explained.

"Back home we don't even have one unicorn, much less three," Alexa said. She patted the rose-colored unicorn on the neck.

"There's one more," Nori continued. "The most powerful of all: the Queen Unicorn."

"She's hidden in another part of the forest, far away from Malucia," Romy added.

Nori scaled a branch and motioned for Alexa to follow. They climbed to the highest platform, and Nori pointed to a large castle looming in the distance. "That's where Malucia lives," she explained.

Alexa marveled at the beautiful castle. It was candy-colored and resting on a double-rainbow bridge. To Alexa, it seemed impossible that a princess would do anything to harm her own kingdom—especially one this breathtaking. Why did Malucia think she needed all the magic for herself?

"She's greedy and deceitful," Nori said softly.

"Wicked and monstrous," added Romy.

Alexa shook her head in disbelief. Royals should protect their kingdoms—not steal from them. But she knew that living up to others' expectations was difficult. Maybe Malucia just needed to find her own path.

One thing was clear: Nori and Romy needed a plan to get Malucia to return the magic to its rightful owners. But how?

Chapter 10

Across the land of Zinnia at the royal castle, Princess Malucia was busy making her own plan. "Nooo!" the ten-year-old princess shouted, standing on her throne, hands on her hips. She wore a sour expression and purple pigtails. "No, no, NO!" She pushed her too-big tiara out of her eyes and stamped her foot.

Several trogs—the princess's monstrous guards—held up an enormous cake for Malucia to inspect. The cake was decorated with a crude icing drawing of the princess herself. The trog chef stood nearby, anxiously awaiting her reaction.

"That doesn't look anything like me!" Malucia shouted. "This has to be the best cake ever in the history of . . . history!" She hopped down from her throne, stopping to check that her golden scepter was still in its cradle. She paced around the cake, examining it. "Is the first layer chocolate?"

"Yes, Your Majesty," replied her trog attendant, Grodlin. He was in charge of the princess while her parents were away. But lately Malucia had been calling all the shots.

"And the second layer's wickleberry?"

"Of course, Your Majesty," Grodlin declared, adjusting his spectacles on his nose.

"Then one red velvet, one more chocolate, and three more wickleberry?" asked Malucia.

Grodlin and the trog chef glanced at each other.

"Uh . . . I—I'm not certain," Grodlin ventured.

"Argh!" Malucia cried, shooting him a dirty look. "Grodlin, I'm about to have *all* the magic in the kingdom. To celebrate, there's going to be a party to honor the greatest, most magical princess ever—ME." She crossed her arms. "So there better be a *perfect* cake. Got it?"

Just then, Sniff and Whiff rolled in, their leathery scales clicking against the stone floor. Behind them, two trog guards carried in a fairy. She flapped her wings, trying to escape, but they held her firmly.

"Your Highness," said the first trog proudly. "We found a youngling fairy in the woods today."

Sniff raised his paw. "Actually," he began smugly, "that 'we' would be *me,* Your Highness. I'm the one who sniffed her out."

"What are you talking about?" Whiff argued. "I was there, too, you know."

Sniff shook his head. "*I* recognized that faint aroma of laydelberry. All fairies have it, and only experts like me can detect it."

Whiff rolled his eyes. "Unbelievable."

"I hope Your Highness is pleased," Sniff said, bowing deeply. "Her name is Nola."

Nola, no bigger than a bird, stared defiantly at Malucia. Her feathery wings quivered with fear and anger. If only she had taken a different way to the grove, she could have avoided the sniffers.

"She is a tiny *snack*," Malucia sneered, looking down her nose at the trembling fairy. "I want the unicorn combo—supersized! Have you found them yet?"

Sniff and Whiff shrugged and pointed to each other.

Malucia tapped her foot impatiently.

"Um, not quite yet," Sniff said. "But we're out there, noses up, twenty-four seven!"

"Well, get going, then," the princess commanded. "And don't come back until you have those unicorns."

Sniff and Whiff bowed their heads and waddled out of the throne room before curling up and rolling away.

Malucia turned her attention to the fairy. "Now. You," she growled.

"Let me go!" Nola said, tussling with the guards.

"You're no unicorn, but you've got magic. And I want it," Malucia declared, standing on her throne again. The trog guards stepped away from Nola as Malucia raised her scepter. Its giant orb began to glow.

"You don't need my magic!" Nola pleaded.

"On the contrary, my winged friend," Malucia replied, pointing the scepter at Nola's wings. "There is nothing more tragic than a princess without magic. So I must take what I need from you. I want it all!"

She aimed her scepter and—*zap!*—a sickly yellow-green ray shot from its orb. It surrounded Nola's wings, sucking the magic from her. Once Nola's wings were completely drained, they disappeared. *Whoosh!*

"My wings!" Nola sobbed, feeling her back where her wings had been. "You're mean."

Malucia's scepter grew larger with Nola's magic. The princess grinned. "No, I'm goal-oriented. Now, where were we with that cake?"

Chapter 11

Back in the treetop fort, the fairies hosted a tea party to celebrate Alexa's arrival. Alexa felt honored and excited. Plus she was having a blast discovering all that her magic could do. She waved her wand and changed both Nori's and Romy's outfits into tea-party dresses. Then she changed their hairstyles.

I'm getting good at this, she thought.

Next, she changed a teacup into a towering chocolate cake. Finally, she raised the teapot into the air with a flick of her wand, making it pour tea on its own!

"I think I like this world," she declared,

jumping from her seat. "I feel like a different girl!" She skipped through the trees, Nori and Romy right behind her.

Alexa climbed a tree to look out over the kingdom. With a touch of her wand she sent a shower of sparkles down from the trees.

"I can do anything because I've got magic!" she called into the air.

She raced off in the direction of the floating lagoon. "Nori, Romy! I've got a great idea!" she called over her shoulder. "I can use my magic to change you back into a fairy and a mermaid."

Nori raised an eyebrow. "Can you do that?" she asked, doubtful.

Romy jumped up and down excitedly. "She's a princess! She can do anything."

Alexa smiled and waved her wand through the air, showering them with sparkles. "It looks like I *can* do anything! Ready?"

Nori and Romy exchanged a glance and then nodded eagerly.

Alexa closed her eyes in concentration.

Romy walked to the edge of the lagoon. She

crouched in diving position. "Okay, I'm ready! These legs are so impractical," she called, closing her eyes.

Alexa aimed her wand and shot a pink beam toward Romy.

Zing!

Romy opened one eye, then another. Her tea-party dress had been replaced by her regular clothes, but she still had legs.

"Hmm," Alexa murmured. "I'll try again." She flicked her wand. Nothing. She turned toward Nori and sent a pink beam of magic in her direction.

Zing!

Nori didn't change either.

"I don't understand," Alexa said. She shook her wand and then aimed it at a nearby flower.

Zing!

The flower bloomed beautifully on command. Alexa scratched her head.

"My magic still works but not on you. And here I thought I was getting really good at this."

Nori put an arm around her shoulder. "You

are. But I guess you can't put back what Malucia has stolen. Maybe it has to come from her."

Romy nodded. "Right from her scepter! That's where our magic is. We get that scepter, we get our magic back."

Nori snapped her fingers, an idea lighting up her eyes. "With a princess on our side, we can fight Malucia and get her scepter!"

Alexa cringed. She understood why Nori and Romy thought she could help. But Alexa wasn't so sure. What if she failed? She felt her old insecurities creeping back.

"Making flowers bloom and changing outfits is one thing, but fighting a magical princess? I can't do it." She hung her head miserably. Maybe things weren't so different here after all.

Chapter 12

At Malucia's castle, a different kind of tea party was about to begin.

"So nice of you to join me at my magical tea party!" Malucia announced from a tiny gold chair at a little table. Three trogs and Nola the fairy sat around the table, looking uncomfortable.

"Did we have a choice?" whispered one trog to the other.

"I didn't," Nola mumbled.

Malucia rapped her scepter on the floor to get everyone's attention.

"We'll start with the pastries. Who wants one?" She pointed toward a plate heaped high with cakes and donuts of every kind.

The trogs reluctantly raised their hands. If Malucia wanted them to have pastries, they knew better than to argue. Nola turned away in protest.

Next, Malucia waved her scepter, causing a teapot to appear out of thin air.

"Tea's done! Boiling hot and ready to drink!" She raised her scepter. "I'll pour."

The trogs eyed the teapot nervously. One false move and they'd be scorched!

Just then Sniff and Whiff rolled in.

Malucia turned her attention to them, momentarily forgetting the teapot. Hot water splashed everywhere. The trogs ran for cover.

"Look what you made me do!" Malucia cried, stamping her foot angrily at the sniffers. "Where is she?"

Whiff spread a large map out on the table. "This is us," he began, pointing to a castle painted on the map. "And this glade is where we *think* the Queen Unicorn may be hiding."

"Only *one* of us thinks that, Your Highness,"

said Sniff. "I'm not picking up anything but stenchweed. LOTS of it."

"That's the point," Whiff replied, rolling his eyes. "Too much of it. Stenchweed doesn't even grow in these parts, see? So I'm thinking, maybe someone put it there on purpose. To hide something big and magical they don't want us to find, like maybe—"

Malucia's eyes grew big. "The Queen Unicorn."

"Your Highness," Whiff continued, stepping forward, "the unicorn is in that grove. I bet my brother on it."

"Excuse me?" Sniff scoffed, offended.

"Good job," Malucia said. Then she studied the map. "Hmm, we need to know *exactly* where that unicorn is."

She looked slyly over her shoulder at Nola. "And I know who knows exactly where it is," she whispered to herself. All she had to do was get Nola to show her where the fairies were hiding the magical creature. Then the Queen Unicorn would fall right into her evil little hands.

Malucia snapped her fingers, calling everyone—but especially Nola—to attention. "So the sniffers found the Queen Unicorn! Oh, goody!" she squealed. "Grodlin! What are you waiting for? Round up the trogs and let's go get her!"

Nola looked up from the table, her brow furrowed with worry.

Malucia bumped into Nola, acting like it was an accident.

"Oh, hi there!" she said innocently. "So, I'm going to let you go. But don't you dare tell *anyone* about me going to capture the Queen Unicorn. Got it?"

"Yes," Nola replied. "Meany," she added under her breath.

Malucia whirled around. "What?"

"Yes, great and powerful princess," Nola replied.

"That's better. Now shoo!" Malucia ordered.

She rubbed her hands together. Now all she needed was for Nola to run home and tell the other fairies. If the fairies knew about Malucia's plan to raid the unicorn's hiding place, they would surely try to move her. And when they did, Malucia would be right there, waiting.

"Let's go get that unicorn!" she commanded the trogs.

Chapter 13

Alexa sat near the lagoon, patting the unicorns. She felt miserable.

What was the point of having magic if she couldn't use it to help her friends? And if she couldn't be helpful, then she should probably just go home. It didn't do any good to get everyone's hopes up.

Nori and Romy sat nearby with other fairies and mermaids, trying to think of a plan to save Zinnia's magic.

Suddenly, Nori cupped a hand to her ear. "Someone's here!" she cried.

They raced to the tree-fort entrance just

Princess Alexa would rather read than learn a new dance for the ball.

Oops! Alexa trips and falls during dance practice.

Alexa's new book unlocks a secret door
in the palace garden.

Alexa meets Romy and Nori in a magical fairyland.

Alexa, Romy, and Nori hide from the sniffers.

Alexa discovers that she has magical powers!

Romy and Nori take Alexa to meet the unicorns.

Princess Malucia is stealing all the magic
in the kingdom.

A fairy tells Alexa that Malucia is on her way to capture
the Queen Unicorn!

Alexa, Romy, and Nori fly off to rescue
the Queen Unicorn.

The Queen Unicorn gives the girls a ride.

Oh no! Malucia captures the Queen Unicorn.

Alexa battles Malucia with magic.

Alexa's magic breaks Malucia's scepter and
defeats the spoiled princess.

Alexa's new friends thank her for restoring
the kingdom's magic.

Alexa goes home and embraces her role as princess
with a dance at the big ball!

in time to see Nola the fairy spring onto the platform.

"Nola!" Nori cried. "Your wings!"

Everyone gasped in despair. Malucia had struck again.

"I had to walk all the way from the castle," Nola replied wearily.

Romy looked alarmed. "Did anyone follow you?"

"No, I don't think so. But they've found the Queen Unicorn," Nola warned. "Malucia's on her way right now to capture her and steal her magic."

"We have to get to the Queen Unicorn! We have to!" Romy shouted in a panic.

Alexa struggled to take it all in. "What will happen if you don't?"

"If Malucia takes the Queen Unicorn's magic, and then gets ahold of these three . . ." She pointed at the other unicorns.

"She'll be unstoppable," Nori explained darkly. Then she jumped into planning mode. "Romy and I will get the Queen Unicorn and bring her here. Everyone else, stay and protect the other unicorns—and each other."

Alexa couldn't take it anymore. What Malucia was doing was wrong. Trying to find one's own path shouldn't mean hurting so many others in the process.

But, Alexa was learning, sometimes it did mean taking risks. She stepped forward. "I'm not sure exactly how I can help, but I'd like to try."

Nori and Romy grinned. The girls high-fived.

"We have to hurry," Romy urged. "Malucia might be there already."

"Of all times not to have wings," Nori moaned.

Alexa looked out across the lagoon. She saw the giant lily pads floating on the water's surface. She had an idea.

"Hey, maybe I *do* know how to help," she started. "Remember the story about the boy and the flying carpet?"

"What's a carpet?" Romy asked.

Alexa giggled. She had forgotten she wasn't

at home anymore. Rather than explain, she aimed her wand at the lily pads. A purple beam of magic surrounded one, lifting it into the air and making it fly toward them.

"Never mind! Get on!" she cried.

The three friends climbed onto the lily pad. Alexa closed her eyes and focused. She flicked her wand and the lily pad started to quiver. She concentrated harder and felt the lily pad rise into the air.

"Whoa!" Romy and Nori cried.

But as quickly as it had risen, the lily pad plopped back down. Alexa blew out a frustrated breath.

"It's too big for me to control. It's not going to work."

"Yes, it will," Romy said.

"Try again," Nori urged.

Alexa squared her shoulders. She was determined to help—and now was the time. She focused her wand's magic beam once more, and the lily pad rose into the air. She steered it right and left, testing it.

When she was sure the lily pad was flight-worthy, Alexa grinned at her friends. "Which way?" she asked.

"Over there!" Romy said, pointing.

With a wave of Alexa's wand, the girls took off! They flew over the mermaid lagoon and past a few hovering fairies, who dropped their jaws in amazement. The girls glided across the countryside, whooping and laughing as they dipped and zipped.

Alexa tipped her head back to feel the breeze on her face.

"This is *almost* as good as having wings!" Nori exclaimed above the rush of wind.

Below them, Alexa spotted a river. She steered the lily pad downward. Romy trailed her fingers in the cool, clean water before they rose into the sky again.

"This is so much fun!" Romy cried.

Alexa beamed. It felt wonderful to see her friends' smiling faces. If only it could last.

Chapter 14

As Malucia's caravan wound its way through the hills toward the unicorn grove, Alexa, Nori, and Romy left their lily pad nearby. They crawled on their bellies to the top of the hill and peered into the valley below.

"The unicorn is down there," Nori whispered.

"But how do we get to her?" Alexa asked. It seemed impossible to enter the grove without being seen. Malucia and her entourage could be on any of the surrounding hills, looking for them.

"I know. We can chop down these trees, build a catapult, and launch ourselves over there," suggested Romy enthusiastically.

Nori raised an eyebrow. "Or there is a secret opening, between those two trees," she said with a wink.

Romy blushed. "That could work, too," she replied sheepishly.

Alexa took a deep breath. She wasn't sure she was ready for such a risky mission. But if she didn't help her friends save the Queen Unicorn, she would never forgive herself. The girls crouched low and raced down the hill toward a cluster of trees.

"Through here," Nori instructed, moving aside some curled-in branches.

Alexa followed her friends through the trees toward a small clearing ahead. Then she stopped in her tracks.

Before her stood the most beautiful creature she had ever seen. Tall and pink, with a glorious rainbow mane and tail, the Queen Unicorn pawed the ground nervously as the girls approached.

Nori placed a gentle hand on the unicorn's muzzle to calm her. "Shhh. It's all right. This is Princess Alexa. She's a friend."

The unicorn moved toward Alexa and nuzzled her. As her iridescent rainbow horn brushed Alexa's shoulder, it started to glow softly.

"Hey!" Romy gasped. "She never does that for us!"

Alexa smiled and patted the Queen Unicorn's neck.

"It's nice to meet you, too," she whispered, hardly believing that such a magnificent creature existed. "But we have to get you out of here."

The unicorn nodded and whinnied softly. Then she trotted toward a nearby tree stump and stopped. She looked at Alexa expectantly.

"I think she wants you to get on," Nori interpreted.

Using the stump for help, Alexa swung her leg across the unicorn's back. But the unicorn didn't budge.

"I think she wants *all* of us," Alexa guessed.

Nori and Romy climbed on. But still the Queen Unicorn didn't move. So they climbed off again. Then the Queen Unicorn took off, leaving them racing behind her!

"I really miss my wings!" Nori said.

"I know, right?" replied Romy, tripping. "Oops—legs!"

The girls reached the unicorn's side, and Alexa helped swing them up.

They raced out of the grove toward their fortress.

High on a hill, Malucia and her troop stood, watching them.

"Just as I thought. Follow them!" the princess ordered.

Chapter 15

As the Queen Unicorn galloped through the forest at breakneck speed, the girls clung to her back. The less time they spent out in the open, the smaller the chance of running into Malucia.

Finally, the Queen Unicorn skidded to a stop at the base of the secret fort's tree. They waited for a platform to descend. Then they could hoist the Queen Unicorn up into the safety of the treetops.

"Wooo," Alexa said, letting out a breath. "I can't believe we did that!"

"Alexa, without you, we wouldn't have made it before Malucia," Nori remarked.

Alexa beamed. Using her magic to ride the lily pad directly to the Queen Unicorn's grove had saved valuable time. "I'm glad I could help."

"Can you imagine the look on Malucia's face when she finds out the unicorn's gone?" Romy said. She put on her best pouty face. "She'll be like 'How did this happen? Where's my unicorn?'"

Alexa and Nori cracked up. It felt good to be back at the fort—and safe. The girls loaded the Queen Unicorn onto the platform. They were about to raise her up when they heard a voice behind them.

"I know *exactly* where my unicorn is!"

Malucia!

The girls spun around to see the princess and her army of trogs. The trogs wheeled a big metal cage behind them.

"They followed us!" Nori cried.

Alexa was still staring at Malucia. All this time she'd been picturing a horrible-looking witch. But the princess standing before her was just a girl—a pouty, purple-haired little girl! It didn't make sense.

"That's Malucia?" Alexa asked. "She looks so—"

"Horrible? Treacherous? Out of control?" Romy suggested.

"I was going to say *small*," Alexa replied.

"Don't let that fool you," cautioned Nori. "As long as she has that scepter, she's dangerous."

Malucia approached them. The girls moved to block the Queen Unicorn.

"Why, hello, whoever you are," Malucia cooed sweetly. "It seems I've already got your magic. So I guess I'll just be taking my unicorn." She aimed her scepter at the Queen Unicorn.

Romy dove, pushing Alexa out of the way. "Alexa, hide!" she cried.

Alexa ran for a thicket of trees.

"Go! Run!" Nori shouted at the Queen Unicorn.

The Queen Unicorn bucked but didn't move fast enough. The trogs lassoed her with ropes—trapping her on the platform.

"Put her in the cage!" Malucia ordered the trogs. "Gently."

Alexa hid behind a large tree trunk. She watched as Nori and Romy leapt onto the platform in front of the unicorn. An army of trogs surrounded the girls.

Nori and Romy fought the trogs as they pushed and pulled the Queen Unicorn into the cage. But it was no use. Two guards grabbed them and held them back.

The girls watched helplessly as the lock on the Queen Unicorn's cage clicked shut.

Alexa saw Malucia sitting high in her carriage, aiming her scepter at the Queen Unicorn. Malucia was about to take the unicorn's magic! Alexa knew she had to act.

She whipped out her wand and shot a blast of magic at a flower near Malucia's carriage. The flower bent back and then—*whack!*—it hit Malucia, knocking her from her carriage.

"Oof! What was *that*?" Malucia cried.

Next, Alexa fired fruit from a nearby tree at the princess.

"Argh!" Malucia screamed, diving behind her carriage. She peeked out and spotted Alexa.

"Who *are* you?" she asked. Then she waved her scepter, causing a branch above Alexa to crash down right next to her.

"Ahh!" Alexa cried, leaping out of the way. She sprinted through the trees.

Malucia took off after her.

Alexa looked over her shoulder as she ran. It was just princess versus princess now.

Chapter 16

Alexa raced through the forest, dodging falling branches as Malucia severed them with her magic.

"I'm the only one who can have magic!" she heard Malucia holler behind her. Then Alexa tripped over a root. Her wand flew through the air and landed in front of her.

Malucia seized her opportunity. She aimed her scepter at Alexa.

A sickly green beam shot toward Alexa, surrounding her. Alexa watched as her pink magic slowly seeped away from her, toward the scepter. The scepter absorbed her magic, growing bigger as Alexa felt weaker. It looked like Malucia would win after all!

But Malucia's wand was now so heavy with magic, the princess had a hard time controlling it. She stumbled and Alexa saw her chance. Summoning the magic she had left, she broke away from Malucia's power. She dashed through the woods, leaving her wand behind.

"Ahhhhh!" Alexa heard Malucia scream with frustration. She kept her head down and ran— away from Malucia, away from the secret fort and toward the one place she knew she'd be safe.

When she turned the corner she saw it: the entrance to the magic tunnel.

Romy and Nori stepped from the platform into the treetop fort, followed closely by the trog guards. Then Malucia herself appeared. She looked around at the fairies and mermaids.

"Hey, you guys are having a party? And you didn't invite me?" Malucia whined.

"That's because you're mean!" one of the fairies shouted.

Malucia cocked her head, amused. "True. Now let's get this party started!" She pointed her scepter at the crowd.

"Ahhhhh!" the creatures shouted as they scattered in all directions.

Alexa ran toward the tunnel as quickly as she could. She paused to catch her breath. All she had to do was get to the royal garden and she'd be safe—back in her own world. She wouldn't have magic there—but she also wouldn't have a greedy princess chasing her.

There was just one problem: she couldn't stop thinking about Nori and Romy. What would happen to them if she left?

It was true that magic had brought Alexa a whole heap of trouble. But it had also given her two friends who believed in her—more than she believed in herself. And that was worth protecting. Before she could change her mind, Alexa turned on her heel and dashed back toward the fortress. If Malucia wanted a battle, she'd show her one.

Chapter 17

Alexa made her way carefully from tree to tree, checking her surroundings to make sure no one saw her. When she made it back to the clearing, she stepped over the splintered tree branches, scouring the ground. Her magic wand had to be around here somewhere.

Aha! She spotted it under a pile of broken branches.

Just then, a bouncy creature hopped over. It picked up her wand and handed it to her before disappearing into the trees.

Alexa giggled. "Thanks!" she called after the fuzzy, adorable creature. Then she gripped her wand and closed her eyes. This was the moment of truth. She aimed the wand at a flower on the ground.

Zap!

The flower changed color on command!

Still got it! Alexa thought, tucking her wand into her hair. It was time to get down to business.

She raced to the fort entrance and pushed a button on the tree trunk to lower the platform. Then she shot a beam of pink magic around it and felt herself rise into the tree. *Here we go!*

When she reached the top, she exited the platform carefully. There was no telling what she might find. The place looked deserted. Where was everyone? Were they safe?

"Romy? Nori? Hello?" she called out cautiously. "Is anybody here?"

A few small fairies and mermaids emerged from between the branches, looking beaten down and broken. Alexa noticed that all of their wings and tails were gone. *Malucia.*

Then Nori and Romy came out of their hiding places, looking dejected. "Malucia took everybody's magic," Nori explained. "And she took the unicorns and left us here."

"Oh no!" Alexa cried in despair. If only she had stayed. Now it was too late.

"Why did you come back?" Romy asked.

Alexa wasn't sure she could fully explain why. "I just had to," she said.

Nori and Romy smiled sadly at her.

Alexa couldn't bear to see her friends so devastated. There had to be something she could do.

"Everyone!" she said, motioning for them all to gather around. "I know you feel helpless right now, but I still have my magic." She made a flower bloom nearby to prove it. "And as long as I do, I promise to do everything I can to get back your magic and the unicorns!"

The fairies and mermaids cheered.

Alexa cautiously eyed Nori and Romy. Would they still want her help even after she had left them? "Feel like another magic carpet ride?" she asked.

Nori and Romy looked at each other and

grinned. "Oh, yeah!" The girls piled onto a lily pad and took off through the air.

Alexa wasn't sure what her plan was or how things would turn out. But if Nori and Romy were willing to take a chance on her, then she had to be willing to take a chance on herself.

Chapter 18

All around them the clouds of Zinnia darkened. The sky flickered each time Malucia sucked magic from another creature. They were running out of time.

Alexa steered the lily pad down toward the castle. They hovered above a domed skylight that offered a view of the throne room.

They peered inside and saw the Queen Unicorn and the smaller unicorns. The magical creatures were chained at their feet and guarded by trogs.

Malucia stood in front of them. She held her scepter high and used it to suck the last of the magic from the unicorns' horns.

"Oh no!" Romy cried as they watched the Queen Unicorn's horn disappear.

"We're too late," Nori moaned.

Inside the throne room, Grodlin and the trogs looked on as Malucia greedily took every last bit of magic from the unicorns.

"That's it," Grodlin said. "She has all the magic." He shook his head.

Even the trogs looked worried.

Malucia, on the other hand, smiled brightly. "Woo-hoo!" she exclaimed. "Now let's pass out the hats and bring on the cake!"

Still hovering above the dome, Alexa, Nori, and Romy wondered what to do next. The air around them flickered and went dark. It seemed as though all the colors had drained from the kingdom—right into Malucia's scepter. Even the rainbow bridges around the castle had faded to black.

"Malucia won," Romy said miserably. "She got it all."

Alexa squared her shoulders. "No," she said firmly. "Not all of it." She pulled out her wand.

"But what can you do?" Nori asked, defeated. "Her magic is too strong now."

"You'll never know what you're good at unless you try," Alexa said, repeating her grandmother's words. She took a deep breath and steered the lily pad toward the castle entrance.

"And now that I have all the magic," Malucia said smugly from her throne, "CAKE!"

Grodlin and the trog chef wheeled out a giant sheet cake covered with white frosting.

"Hold on!" Malucia barked, examining the cake. "Where's my picture?"

"Your Majesty, no cake decorator is equal to the task of drawing your portrait," the trog chef gushed. "The only person who could do justice to the princess is the princess herself."

Malucia considered this. "You're right!" Then she aimed her scepter at the cake. "A self-portrait in blue icing!" she ordered.

Zap!

A picture of the princess appeared on the cake—perfectly centered.

Malucia looked shocked—she rarely got it right on the first try.

"I did it!" she cried delightedly. "I can do anything now! All I needed was *enough* magic!" She aimed her scepter at the ceiling.

Boom!

A shower of fireworks sparkled through the air. "Hoo-hoo!" Next she made a shimmering disco ball appear on the ceiling, followed by a unicorn piñata.

Grodlin furrowed his brow. There really was no stopping her now.

Chapter 19

Alexa peered around the corner at the castle's main entrance. Two imposing trog guards blocked the door.

I guess there's only one way to do this, Alexa thought. She motioned for Nori and Romy to follow her and walked confidently toward the door.

"Excuse me?" she said to the guards sweetly.

The trogs looked startled. "What? Er. Who goes there?"

Alexa gathered her courage. "We wish to formally surrender to the great and powerful Malucia."

The trogs looked at each other, trying to decide if Alexa was telling the truth. No one had ever surrendered to Malucia. But then again, the princess had *all* of the magic now, so maybe it made sense. "Oh, all right," said one. "This way."

The guards led Alexa, Nori, and Romy down a castle hallway, toward the throne room and Malucia.

"They put up quite a fight, Your Highness," a trog guard shouted over the noise of the princess's fireworks.

"Good work, guys!" Malucia exclaimed. She stopped the fireworks and sat in her throne. "I remember you two." She eyed Nori and Romy and laughed meanly. "But you," she said, shaking her scepter at Alexa. "You're not a fairy or a mermaid."

"I'm a princess," Alexa said proudly.

"Right," Malucia scoffed. "*I'm* the only princess around here. I bet you don't even have real magic. Sniffers!"

At Malucia's command, Sniff and Whiff wobbled into the room. They sniffed around

Alexa's feet, checking for magic. "That's the most magic I've smelled—ever!" Sniff exclaimed.

"Holy moly! My nose is going to explode!" Whiff cried.

"Duh!" Malucia said. "I just took the magic from everybody—and the four unicorns."

Sniff shook his head. "No, Your Highness, not you." He pointed at Alexa. "Her!"

Furious, Malucia pointed her scepter at Sniff.

Whiff leapt in front of his brother to protect him. "Sniff, tell the nice princess that she's still the most magical creature in the *whoooole* kingdom, right?" he instructed, urging his brother to agree.

Sniff looked confused. "No! Yeah!" he stammered. "Of course," he said, catching on. "The most magical creature . . ."

The sniffers bolted from the room before Malucia could punish them further.

Malucia walked in a circle around Alexa. "Okay, Your Highness," she sneered. "Apparently you're not up on all of the latest princess rules. Like how no one gets to have magic in this kingdom except me." She glared at Alexa.

Alexa took a deep breath. "I'll make a deal with you," she said bravely.

"What kind of deal?" asked Malucia, watching her suspiciously.

"Give everyone their magic back, and I'll let you go," Alexa answered, returning Malucia's stare.

Malucia looked shocked and then she let out an evil laugh. "You? *You'll* let *me* go? That's really funny!" She turned to her trog army. "Isn't that funny?"

The trogs forced a few laughs.

But then Malucia turned serious. She whipped her scepter toward Alexa. It was so heavy with magic, she almost tipped over. "Sorry, missy, but all the magic is mine!"

Reacting fast, Alexa plucked her wand from her hair. She pointed it toward a shield on the wall. The shield flew in front of her just as Malucia's green ray of magic blasted toward her. The green ray bounced off of the shield and right back at the scepter, knocking it out of

Malucia's hand and causing her to fall down!

"Oof!" Malucia cried. She scrambled to her feet and climbed on top of a nearby table. "All right, princess imposter-pants. Let's see what you got!"

Alexa aimed her wand at the floor below Malucia. *Poof!* A plant shot out of the ground.

Malucia crossed her arms. "Impressive," she said sarcastically.

Suddenly, Alexa's plant started to grow. It sent out dozens of long, spindly tendrils that twisted and coiled, reaching for Malucia.

Malucia jumped, trying to avoid a tentacle wrapping around her ankle. But another one wrapped itself around her scepter, pulling it away from her. "Give me that!" the princess yelled, yanking it back. She aimed it at the ceiling and a cloud formed. Snow fell from the cloud, blanketing the plant. The tendrils shrank back from the cold and the plant started to wither.

Frustrated, Malucia pointed her scepter at the disco ball overhead. It spun faster and faster until it came unbolted from the ceiling.

Whizz! The ball flew through the air, careening toward Alexa.

Thinking quickly, Alexa aimed her wand toward the ceiling. A pink beam shot toward the disco ball, severing it from its cord. The shimmering ball smashed into the unicorn piñata hanging right over Malucia's head. The piñata splintered and a shower of candy rained down, burying the princess!

The trogs rushed forward at the sight of all the delicious candy.

"Woo-hoo!" one cried.

"Out of the way! These are the tasty bits!" shouted another.

"Drop that candy—it's mine!" Malucia shouted from underneath the pile of candy. Reluctantly, the trogs inched back to their guard posts, shoving sweets into their pockets.

Alexa watched as Malucia's scepter rose through the pile of candy. Malucia waved it around. All at once, the greedy princess shot out of the candy. She had grown to four times her normal size! Her head almost hit the ceiling.

Nori and Romy gasped in fear.

"*Now* you've done it!" gigantic Malucia roared, glaring at Alexa. "You've ruined my party!" She aimed her scepter at Alexa and a ring of green magic surrounded her.

Chapter 20

Alexa fought with all her might against Malucia's power. Finally, she broke free and fell to the floor. Malucia tried to crush her with the heel of her scepter, but Alexa rolled away.

Grodlin stepped in front of the greedy princess. "Your Highness, you have enough magic," he said, trying to intervene.

Malucia shot a blast of magic at Grodlin, sending him across the room. He landed with a thud next to Nori and Romy.

"Anyone else got something to say?" the princess thundered, waving her bulging scepter through the air.

Alexa studied the scepter closely. Was it just her, or was it so full of magic that it was starting to crack? It was literally bursting at the seams!

Alexa bit her lip in thought. If she could pump Malucia's scepter full of more magic than it could handle, it would break and they could defeat her! It was risky. But if Alexa didn't try, Malucia would win.

Alexa took a deep breath and then jumped to her feet.

"Hey, Malucia!" she shouted. "You want all the magic? Take it!"

Malucia paused, confused. Then a wicked grin spread across her face. She raised her scepter and shot a beam of green magic toward Alexa.

The beam struck Alexa, forcing her backward. Her own pink magic mingled with Malucia's and traveled toward the scepter.

The scepter grew brighter and brighter as more magic flowed into its bulb. Then it began to shake so much that Malucia had trouble controlling it. She held on tight with both hands.

Alexa watched as the crack in the orb grew

bigger and bigger. She felt herself weakening as the magic drained out of her.

But with one final burst of strength, she raised her wand. It faded and disappeared into thin air, gobbled up by the green magic.

Alexa felt faint. She could hardly keep her eyes open. Then she heard the sound she had hoped for.

Kaboom!

Malucia's scepter exploded. The princess flew backward and landed against the wall with a thud.

An explosion of multicolored swirls flew toward Alexa. Brilliant colors surrounded her, hiding her from sight. The crowd gasped as the glittering magic swelled and spun around Alexa.

Then, just as quickly as it began, the spiraling magic softened and slowed.

Alexa emerged from the cloud and blinked, trying to clear her head. She looked down and discovered that she was wearing a magnificent ball gown! The gown, bursting with color and flowers, matched the landscape of Zinnia!

Alexa twirled, admiring its beauty, and felt the luxurious fabric between her fingers. Then she lifted her hand. Even her magic wand had been returned to her!

Alexa waved her wand through the air, as if she couldn't quite believe it belonged to her once more. Then she noticed that all eyes were on her. Grodlin, Nori, Romy, the unicorns, and even the trogs stared at her. They marveled at her beauty and wondered what she would do next.

Alexa didn't have to think twice. She raised her wand and aimed it at Nori. A stream of pink magic shot through the air and instantly restored the fairy's glittering wings.

Alexa grinned. Her plan had worked! Not only was Malucia's scepter shattered, but all of its magic had been transferred to Alexa's wand! And Alexa knew just what to do with it.

Next, she shot a stream of magic toward Romy. *Poof!*

"Tail!" Romy cried, flapping her shimmering mermaid tail with delight.

Alexa aimed another shower of pink magic toward each unicorn, restoring their magic— and their horns.

Then she sent streams of color out the doors and windows, spreading through the palace. The swirls of pink raced through the land of Zinnia, restoring magic wherever it had disappeared. The skies brightened, rainbow bridges glittered once more, and the landscape breathed new life.

A ribbon of magic shot through the trees to the fairies' secret fort. Excited cries echoed throughout the kingdom as mermaids and fairies received their rightful magic.

Then Grodlin stepped forward and bowed. "Thank you, Your Majesty," he said.

"Don't mention it," Alexa replied graciously. She walked toward Romy, who was sitting on the edge of a fountain. "Your tail! It's amazing!" she cried, watching the scales twinkle in the light like diamonds.

"Thank you!" Romy exclaimed, splashing her magnificent, shimmery tail in the water.

"You gave up your magic for us," Nori said.

Alexa smiled. "I would do anything to see you with your beautiful wings," she said.

Nori grinned and took off flying around the room.

Alexa felt lighter than air seeing her friends restored to their original selves.

There is nothing more magical than true friendship, she thought.

The friends linked arms and flew out of the castle on the lily pad, eager to leave Malucia behind. Together with the unicorns, they took off toward the treetop fort.

Chapter 21

When Alexa arrived at the fort, all of the fairies and mermaids clapped and cheered for her.

"Thank you for helping us!" they shouted.

Alexa waved to them all. Then Nori and Romy tackled her in a giant group hug.

I've got all the magic I need, Alexa thought, looking around. Still, she couldn't help but wonder: *What happened to Malucia?*

Back at the castle, Grodlin crossed his arms and smiled as he watched Malucia sweep up the giant mess she had made. In the center of the throne room, the pile of candy and toys she had conjured up with her magic grew larger with each push of the greedy princess's broom.

Then a voice boomed from the doorway. "We're home!"

Grodlin looked up to see the king and queen waltz across the throne room floor.

Malucia dropped her broom and raced toward them. "Mommy! Daddy!" she cried.

"Did you miss us, sweetums?" the king said, hugging his little girl.

"Were you a good girl for Grodlin while we were away?" the queen asked.

Malucia batted her eyelashes innocently. "Yessss," she said, shooting a sideways glance at Grodlin.

"Ahem!" Grodlin said, clearing his throat.

The king crossed his arms. "Oh, Malucia," he said, chuckling with amusement. "Did you try and take over the kingdom again?"

Malucia shuffled her foot back and forth. "Nooooo."

"Malucia," the queen prodded.

"Maybe," Malucia admitted with a sigh.

"Well," the king began. "We'll deal with that—after we give you your present!"

Malucia gave an excited gasp and followed her parents as they glided toward the door.

But she didn't get very far before Grodlin stepped in front of her. He handed her the broom. Malucia sighed and returned to her sweeping. Grodlin stifled a smile. The magnificent land of Zinnia had been restored. And that was the sweetest victory of all.

After celebrating at the tree fort with all of their friends, Nori, Romy, and the Queen Unicorn escorted Alexa back to the tunnel entrance. Alexa wasn't sure she was ready to leave such dear friends, but she knew she had unfinished business at home. It was time to go.

"Don't forget us," Nori pleaded, stepping forward to hug Alexa.

"Never," Alexa replied. She knelt next to the stream that Romy swam in. "I guess you don't miss your legs," she said to the mermaid.

Romy laughed. "Not one bit. Come back and visit us?"

"I will," Alexa promised. Then she patted the Queen Unicorn's muzzle. "Thank you," Alexa whispered quietly.

The unicorn nuzzled her back, her horn aglow.

Alexa gave everyone a final wave and then headed into the tunnel to go home.

Chapter 22

Alexa pushed open the secret door, sparkles swirling around her just as they had before. She stepped into the castle garden and watched as the door disappeared behind her.

It felt wonderful to be back in such a familiar setting. Alexa noticed that she still wore the magnificent ball gown from her time in Zinnia. She grinned broadly, grateful for such a magical souvenir.

Alexa found the book her grandmother had given her lying on the ground just where she'd left it. She picked it up and hugged it to her chest as she made her way along the path. Then she heard a familiar voice calling her name.

"Princess Alexa! Princess Alexa!"

"Over here, Brookhurst!" Alexa called to her butler.

"Ah, there you are, Your Highness," Brookhurst said, practically running into her. "Your mother thought perhaps you were still in your room, reading." He paused, taking in Alexa's stunning gown. "What a lovely dress!"

Alexa grinned. "Thank you."

"I thought I'd better alert you," the butler continued. "The Young Equestrians have gathered on the North Lawn. You may want to take another path back to the palace."

"Oh," Alexa said, cocking her head in thought. "No, Brookhurst. I'd like to see them."

Brookhurst gave her a puzzled look.

"And speak to them!" Alexa added.

"You do?" Brookhurst asked.

Alexa nodded. "I want to try."

"Are you feeling well? Fever, perhaps?" Brookhurst pressed.

"I'm fine, Brookhurst," Alexa replied, laughing.

The truth was, she felt better than fine. She felt like herself—and it was time to show the world just how beautiful she was.

Alexa stood at a podium on the palace's North Lawn. She looked out at the sea of young girls in riding attire, staring back at her.

"Hi," she started, speaking shyly into the microphone. "Thanks for asking me to speak today."

"She's so cool!" one girl shouted in the crowd.

"This is so exciting!" said another.

In the back of the audience, Alexa spotted her mother and grandmother watching her. Her mother looked shocked. But her grandmother looked proud. Seeing her grandmother's face gave Alexa the tiny bit of courage she needed to keep going.

"I'm going to speak to my parents about letting your club use the royal stables to give riding lessons to all the children of our kingdom."

The crowd broke into applause.

One of the horses stepped forward and nuzzled the princess.

This feels familiar, Alexa thought, remembering the unicorns. She patted the horse's mane and the crowd laughed. Alexa grinned.

"Where did she get that dress?" Alexa heard her mother ask.

Her grandmother just flashed a knowing smile.

Chapter 23

A short while later, Alexa approached the parlor doors. If she hurried, she could still catch the Prince of Hilgovia during his visit. She opened the door and peeked her head in. "I hope I'm not interrupting," she called.

Her father, the king, was chatting with the ambassador and his son, the prince. Her mother and grandmother sat across from them.

"Alexa?" the king said, surprised to see his daughter. "This is the ambassador and Prince Kieran."

"It's very nice to meet you," Alexa said, shaking his hand. "What do you like to do in Hilgovia?"

"I like to ride horses, and fence, and I love to read," the prince replied.

"What's gotten into her?" Alexa heard her mother whisper.

"Perhaps it's something she read," her grandmother replied with a wink.

That night in her room, Alexa readied herself for the royal ball. She felt nervous but ready. Her time in Zinnia had taught her that everyone had magic—but it was what you did with it that made you special. And even though she might not always know what she was best at, she was no longer afraid to try.

There was a knock on her door, and then her grandmother entered. "How do I look?" her grandmother asked, giving a twirl. She was wearing a multicolored, iridescent gown— almost the same as the one Alexa wore.

"Magical!" Alexa replied. "Oh, I finished your book."

"And?"

"You know exactly what I like," Alexa said, and they both laughed.

Alexa pulled on her elbow-length gloves and straightened her twinkling tiara. It was time to dance.

Outside the ballroom, Alexa took a final deep breath. Then Brookhurst opened the set of double doors in front of them and announced loudly, "Ladies and gentlemen, King Terrance, Queen Adrienne, and Princess Alexa."

Alexa swept into the ballroom behind her parents. She saw an orchestra playing at one end of the room and guests gathered all over.

Across the dance floor, she spotted the ambassador and the prince. Jenna and Samantha were there, too, dressed in their ball gowns.

"Good evening, everyone," the king welcomed the crowd. "As is our tradition, we'll start the festivities with the Royal Waltz. Tonight, I will be accompanied by my daughter, Princess Alexa."

Alexa heard the music rise and saw Mr. Primrose, her dance instructor, sitting nervously on the sidelines. She took a deep breath, clasped her father's hands, and began to dance.

She moved effortlessly across the floor, gliding and twirling as if she'd been dancing her whole life. Jenna, Samantha, and their partners followed in step next to them. Alexa felt like she was living a dream!

"I think Prince Kieran would like to dance with you," the king said, spotting him across the floor.

Alexa smiled and waved at the prince. "Maybe another time. I'm perfectly happy dancing with you," she said, kissing her father on the cheek. Then she got an idea. "But if it's okay, there's actually another dance I'd like to do."

Her father nodded, and Alexa caught Jenna's and Samantha's eyes. "Come on!" she mouthed.

The three girls zipped out a side door, leaving the guests wondering where they had gone.

But they didn't have to wonder for long because the girls bounced back into the room, dressed in more modern, frilly, short dresses.

Alexa signaled the band to stop playing. Jenna

cued up their dance track. One, two, three, dance!

The girls moved around the room, electrifying the crowd. Alexa hit every step and felt joy spread through her whole body.

She couldn't believe she was up here—in front of the whole kingdom—doing something she had never done before! And it felt great! In fact, it felt magical! There was just no other word to describe it.

Magic. And Alexa knew a thing or two about that. She had traveled to a magical land and back again to discover that the right path for her had been in her very own backyard all along! She just needed a little courage—and the support of her family and friends—to follow it. Her eyes sparkling with happiness, Alexa curtsied to her kingdom and grinned.

It was good to be a princess.

Sing along to these songs from the movie!

What's Gonna Happen

by Gabriel Mann, Amy Powers, and Rob Hudnut

from "Barbie™ and the Secret Door"

[Verse 1]
All I really wanna do is stay right here
Away from prying eyes
'Cause I really gotta get to chapter three
And see if I'm surprised
Will the princess slay the dragon
Will she save the day
Will she find a brand-new world
That takes her breath away

[Chorus]
What's gonna happen
I can't wait to see
What's gonna happen
It's all a mystery
I need to turn the page
Prepare to be amazed

See if she's got it made
Whoa-ah-ah-ah-oh
It's nothing I'd expect
What's gonna happen next

[Verse 2]
All I really wanna do is hide right here
And start on chapter four
Maybe this is where the princess saves her friends
And claims her just reward
Will she shoot a
Perfect arrow
Will her aim be true
Will she meet a mighty foe
And know just what to do

[Chorus]
What's gonna happen
I can't wait to see
What's gonna happen
It's all a mystery

I need to turn the page
Prepare to be amazed
See if she's got it made
Whoa-ah-ah-ah-oh
It's nothing I'd expect
What's gonna happen next

[Bridge]
What if I
Could just dive inside
I could stand tall and it all would come easy to me
Like a dream

[Chorus]
What's gonna happen
I can't wait to see
What's gonna happen
It's all a mystery
Oh-u-ah-ah-ah-oh
I need to turn the page
Prepare to be amazed
See if she's got it made
Whoa-ah-ah-ah-oh
It's nothing I'd expect
What's gonna happen next

If I Had Magic

by Gabriel Mann, Amy Powers, and Rob Hudnut

from "Barbie™ and the Secret Door"

[Verse 1]
My bed would make itself
New books on every shelf
And then I'd cast a spell, abracadabra
My pets would talk to me
And then we'd all have tea
Create a pair of shoes
That would know all the moves
I'd always find the groove, feel the beat now
And with the spotlight on
I'd twirl perfectly

[Chorus]
If I had magic
Magic, magic
If I had magic
Magic, magic

[Verse 2]
I'd make a chocolate lake
Turn cabbage into cake

I'd text without mistakes, LOL yeah
I'd dream a pair of wings
And I would fly away
I'd zoom across the sky
Make it snow in July
I wouldn't be so shy, "pleased to meet you"
I'd do just what I want
Like every single day
Hey-hey-ey

[Chorus]
If I had magic
Magic, magic
If I had magic
Magic, magic

[Bridge]
And I could do anything
Suddenly I would be
Everything that I dreamed I could be

[Chorus]
If I had magic
Magic, magic
If I had magic

Magic, magic
If I had magic
Magic, magic
If I had magic
Magic, magic
Magic, magic
If I had magic
Magic, magic
If I had magic

My Secret Story

Use these pages to write your own story about
what happens when Alexa opens the secret door!

_____

_____

_____

_____

_____

_____

_____

_____

_____

_____

_____

_____

_____

_____

_____

_____

_____

_____

_____

_____

_____

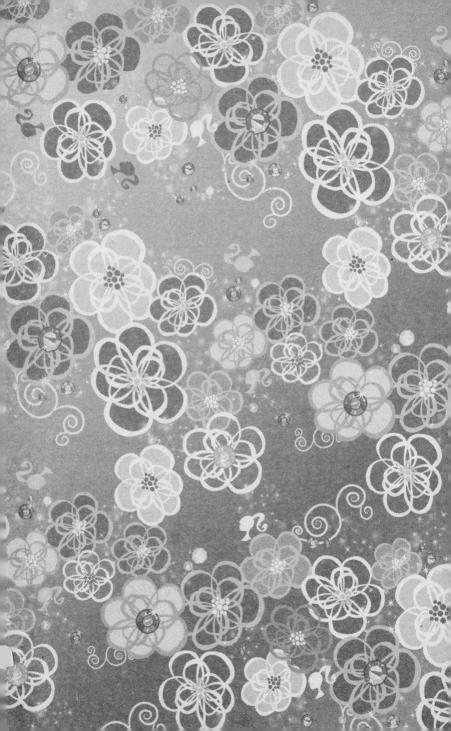